PONY❤DAYS

SHELTIE
the
Hero

D0027078

Read all about Sheltie in these other Pony Days Books!

Sheltie Goes to School

Sheltie in Double Trouble

Sheltie and the Snow Pony

PONY♥DAYS

SHELTIE the Hero

by Peter Clover

Cover illustration by
Tristan Elwell

AN
APPLE
PAPERBACK

SCHOLASTIC INC.
New York Toronto London Auckland Sydney
Mexico City New Delhi Hong Kong Buenos Aires

ISBN 0-439-68888-4

Copyright © 1998 by Working Partners Ltd.
Created by Working Partners Ltd, London W6 OQT.

12 11 10   9/0

Printed in the U.S.A.   40

First Scholastic printing, December 2004

For Ben, Rod, Benjamin, and Peter

Chapter One

"Do you know where you're going yet?" asked Sally.

"No," answered Emma. "It's still a big surprise!"

"Is Sheltie going with you? I bet he is!" added Sally.

Sheltie pricked up his ears when he heard his name.

"Of course!" said Emma. "Sheltie's part of the family. We're all going!" Emma leaned forward and rubbed the little Shetland pony's thick mane.

Emma's dad was planning a special surprise for Mom. It was Mom's birthday that week, and Dad was taking them all away for a short break somewhere as a birthday present.

Emma and Sally had come home from school, finished their snack, and were now having a gentle ride with Sheltie and Minnow, Sally's pony. They were ambling along a bridle path on top of the meadows, watching the clouds drift across the sky, and talking about the special vacation surprise.

"This time tomorrow we'll be there, wherever it is," said Emma. She could hardly wait to see Mom's face when she got back to the house. Dad had promised to spring the surprise on her before they all went to bed.

Emma was excited just thinking about it.

"How will you get there?" asked Sally. Secretly, Emma's best friend was wishing that she was going, too.

"We're taking the car," said Emma, "and Mrs. Linney is bringing the trailer over for Sheltie first thing in the morning."

"I bet it's going to be the beach," said Sally. "It might even be Summerland Bay again! You had a great trip there, didn't you?"

Emma's eyes lit up at the thought of it. "Wherever it is, it will be fantastic," said Emma. "Dad's really good at planning surprises."

Sheltie tossed his head in the air and gave Minnow a friendly nudge with his nose as if to say, "I'm going somewhere special tomorrow!"

Emma and Sally made their way slowly back down to Little Applewood. Then they went their own separate ways as Sally took Minnow home and Emma rode Sheltie back to her house.

"Have a great time!" called Sally over her shoulder as she waved good-bye.

"We will," said Emma. Sheltie blew a noisy raspberry and Minnow flicked his ears back before answering with a soft whicker.

Back in the paddock, Emma untacked Sheltie and settled him down for the night. Then she made sure that everything Sheltie needed for the weekend was ready to be loaded into his trailer the following morning. She measured out enough pony mix for three days into a sack and put his special grooming kit into a bag that Dad had hidden in the tack room.

When Emma skipped into the kitchen,

both Mom and Dad were sitting at the table having a cup of tea. Emma's baby brother, Joshua, had already been tucked in bed upstairs and was fast asleep.

As soon as Emma saw Mom, she started to smile. Dad grinned, too, and gave Emma a special look.

"What's going on between you two?" said Mom. She could tell that they were both keeping something from her.

"Should we tell her now, Emma?" said Dad.

"Tell me what?" Mom smiled. "What are you two up to?"

Emma could hardly keep the secret a moment longer. She felt that any minute she would blurt out the surprise.

"Well," began Dad, "as a special

birthday treat I'm taking us all away for a little vacation. You deserve a break, and it will be nice for us to go somewhere for a few days."

"What a wonderful surprise!" said Mom. "And how long have you known about this, Emma?"

"Oh, ages," chirped Emma. "But I didn't spoil it and say anything, did I?"

"No, you didn't." Mom laughed. "And I can normally tell when you're trying to keep a secret."

"She's been absolutely great," said Dad. Emma felt her face turn red.

"And where are we going, then? Do you know that as well, Emma? Or is that a surprise to both of us?" said Mom.

"You'll both find out when we get there,"

said Dad. "And not a moment before. The best part of a surprise is making it last as long as possible."

Emma couldn't wait for tomorrow to come. For once, she went to bed early without complaining, just so that the morning would come even quicker.

Chapter Two

The next morning, Emma woke to the
sound of the rooster crowing in Mr.
Brown's meadow. It was still very early,
but when Emma rushed to the window
and looked out, she saw that Sheltie was
already wide awake, too.

But he wasn't waiting by the paddock
gate this morning. He was busy being
petted by Mrs. Linney across the top of the
wooden fence. Sheltie used to belong to

Mrs. Linney and she was now a good friend of the family.

Mrs. Linney had come to help Dad with his surprise and had brought along a little Sheltie-sized trailer. The trailer stood like a tiny house on wheels in the driveway.

Emma threw open her bedroom window and called out to Mrs. Linney. As soon as Sheltie heard Emma's voice, he looked up excitedly and did his funny stomping dance. Then he called to Emma with a loud "good morning" whinny.

Emma dressed quickly and made her bed before rushing downstairs and out into the yard. It was time for Sheltie's breakfast.

"I bet you're really excited, too, aren't you, Sheltie?" said Mrs. Linney. "I wish I was coming with you."

After Emma had fed Sheltie, Mom and Dad came out of the house with Joshua. When Joshua saw Sheltie's trailer, he realized that they were going somewhere and jumped up and down so hard that he fell over and sat down with a bump.

"Come on, Joshua," said Emma. "Come upstairs and help me pack." She took Joshua's hand and led him inside.

When Emma had finished, Dad loaded all the bags into the trunk of their car and then put Sheltie's things into the trailer.

Mrs. Linney waited by the driveway as they set off. Sheltie stood inside the trailer looking through the little window at the front. Emma sat with Joshua in the backseat of the car and waved as they pulled out into the road.

"Have a nice weekend!" called Mrs. Linney. She watched as they disappeared up the road.

"This is the best surprise ever, isn't it?" said Emma. Her eyes sparkled almost as brightly as Sheltie's.

Mom reached back and ruffled Emma's hair.

"It's a wonderful surprise, Emma. And wherever it is that we're going, it will be the best birthday present I could possibly wish for."

An hour later, Emma asked, "Where *are* we going, Dad?"

"Not telling you," answered Dad cheerfully. "You'll all see when we get there."

Emma and Mom smiled at each other. Joshua was fast asleep and strapped safely into his booster seat. Emma looked around and saw Sheltie peering through his little window.

"I bet Sheltie knows where we're going," said Emma.

"I bet he doesn't." Dad laughed.

Emma sank back in her seat and hugged her knees. She liked surprises. She decided to play a game and tried to guess where they were going.

"Is it Summerland Bay?" she asked.

"No," said Dad, "but I'll give you one clue. It's somewhere we've never been before!"

Emma laughed. "That's not much of a clue, is it? How can I possibly guess where it is if I've never been there before?"

"Try harder," said Dad.

Emma looked around at all the countryside they were passing through. Flat open fields stretched away in every direction. "Is it a farm vacation?" she asked.

"No," said Dad.

14

"Is it a camping trip?"

"No, but you're getting warm," said Dad.

"How warm?" asked Emma, laughing.

"Very warm," said Dad.

"It's a camp, isn't it?" said Emma.

"It's not," said Dad. "But you'll find out soon. We're almost there."

Up ahead, Emma suddenly saw the sea in the distance as they came over the top of a hill. The water sparkled like diamonds on a mirror beneath the blue sky.

Sheltie could smell the sea air as they headed down toward the coast, and Emma heard him whinny softly. Then suddenly, Dad pulled the car over and drove up in front of a farmhouse.

"Here we are," said Dad. "Out you go!"

"Is this where we're staying?" said Emma. "It *is* a farm vacation."

"No it's not." Dad grinned. "Now, let's go!"

Then Mom and Emma both saw it at the same time.

A brightly colored carriage stood in the far corner of the yard, with its two harness poles sticking out in front, resting on the ground.

"It's a carriage trip," said Dad. "We're going to travel the countryside and go wherever we like."

Emma hopped from one foot to the other. The horse-drawn carriage looked a little like Todd Wallace's old carriage, but larger.

"Is Sheltie going to pull it?" asked

Emma. The carriage seemed far too heavy
for Sheltie. Emma was worried.

"No," said Dad. "We've got a special
horse for that job."

"A *horse*!" chirped Emma. "Where? Can I
go look?" She was so excited.

"Yes," said Dad. "Just a quick look, Emma, and then come help us carry our things."

Emma ran to the back of the farm buildings and saw the horse in its stable. It was a huge brown-and-white carthorse, far bigger than Emma could ever have imagined. The name TOBY was painted on the stable door in green letters.

Emma raced back to the trailer to tell Sheltie.

"Just wait until you see Toby," said Emma. "He's a giant!"

Sheltie shuffled in his trailer and blew a snort as Emma helped Dad to lead him out.

18

Chapter Three

The farmer came over to greet them and they all stood and took a closer look at the carriage. It was beautifully painted with swirly blue-and-green patterns.

There were red-checked curtains above the half door at the back, and green-checked curtains across the small window at the front. Inside there was a stove, a table with two long bench seats on each side that could be made into tiny beds, and two bunks at the back.

Emma tethered Sheltie to a ring on the side of the carriage and helped to carry things inside. Dad brought the suitcases, then went with the farmer to get Toby.

When Sheltie saw Toby, his ears pricked up right away. The carthorse towered above the little Shetland pony. Sheltie looked up with his big brown eyes and raised one hoof. Toby looked down and blew softly through his thick lips. Then very gently, he nuzzled the top of Sheltie's head.

Sheltie whickered softly and rubbed himself against Toby's huge legs. Sheltie had never seen such an enormous animal before.

"I think those two have made friends already," said Mom. She held Joshua in her

arms and lifted him high to pat Toby's
shaggy neck.

"He's a real gentle giant," said the
farmer. "A bit lazy, mind you. But a real old
character. Quiet as a lamb."

"But he's as big as an elephant!" Emma
laughed.

Emma watched the farmer show Dad how to harness Toby to the poles, then she helped to store his hay and feed on hooks at the back of the carriage. Finally, they were ready.

Emma held Toby's bridle and talked to him while she stroked his soft muzzle, reaching up to pat his enormous neck. Toby was so big, she couldn't reach anywhere near his ears.

Suddenly, Toby shifted position and looked around for Sheltie.

"Dad," called Emma. "He's moving!"

"Don't worry," said Dad. "He can't go far — the brake's on." Dad took the reins and climbed up into the driver's seat. Mom climbed up, too, and sat Joshua in between them.

"You can ride Sheltie and lead the way, Emma!" said Dad, smiling.

"This is awesome!" said Emma as she quickly tacked up. "Follow the leader. But you'll have to tell me which way to go!"

Dad waved his map and called, "Straight ahead." He pulled up the brake and jangled Toby's reins. The carriage rolled forward.

Emma was glowing with pride as Sheltie walked on, leading Toby down the dirt roads. The sun shone brightly and a gentle breeze blew Sheltie's long mane out to the side.

Toby couldn't take his eyes off his new little friend. And if Sheltie stopped for a moment, then Toby stopped, too. When Sheltie blew a snort, Toby answered with a deep whinny.

"They are funny, aren't they?" said Mom, laughing. Emma giggled and leaned forward to give Sheltie a kiss.

Dad handled the driving really well, especially as he had been given only a quick five-minute lesson by the farmer.

Then Mom took a turn. Emma and Sheltie pranced alongside Toby. Sheltie was really showing off and lifting his hooves extra high, like a show pony. He was enjoying every minute of this special vacation.

Although Toby was really strong and could pull the carriage easily along the flat, straight roads, he was very lazy. He kept stopping every now and then for a sudden snatch of grass. That was when Sheltie helped by standing in front and blowing snorts to encourage Toby to keep going.

But if Emma and Sheltie went too far
ahead, Toby would stop again and refuse
to budge until Sheltie came back.

"It looks as though Sheltie is in charge,"
said Mom. "It seems that Toby won't go
anywhere without him."

Sheltie, on the other hand, went everywhere that Emma asked him to, and was happy to trot just ahead of his new giant friend, leading the way.

When they finally stopped for the day, they made their camp in a beautiful spot overlooking the bay. Emma asked if she could take Sheltie for a ride.

"I won't go far," she said. "Just around a little to explore."

But Toby hated being left behind. Mom had to distract Toby with a carrot while Emma led Sheltie away. When they were far enough away, she mounted Sheltie where Toby couldn't see them.

The countryside was beautiful, with cliff-top views across the bay.

Emma rode Sheltie for half an hour and explored the first part of the next day's route.

Dad had told Emma that in the morning they were going to make their way slowly down to the sea and follow the coast road. And again Sheltie would be leading the way. Emma felt very important, just like an explorer.

That evening, Dad hammered a big peg into the grass and tethered Toby and Sheltie on lead ropes to graze while Mom

made their dinner in the carriage. Emma
sorted out Sheltie's and Toby's feeds and
scattered some hay on the ground. Then
she gave them a drink in a plastic bucket
that she filled from the carriage's water
tank.

"It feels like a real adventure," said
Emma, peeping out over the half door to

watch Sheltie and Toby. "This is the best vacation ever!"

Mom agreed and gave Dad a hug.

They ate their dinner and Emma was allowed to stay up late and watch the stars appear before bedtime. She couldn't wait to tell Sally all about it. She made sure she remembered every detail of the first day by going over it in her head at least three times before she finally fell asleep in her cozy little bed.

Chapter Four

The next morning started with a real
panic. Emma woke to the sound of Dad's
voice outside the carriage calling, "They're
gone. Sheltie and Toby are gone!"

Emma couldn't believe her ears. She
leaped out of bed and rushed outside,
still in her pajamas. Joshua stayed tucked
in bed, sleeping.

Dad stood scratching his head, staring at
the spot where the big wooden peg had

30

been. But the peg that Sheltie and Toby had been tethered to was gone. And so were Sheltie and Toby.

"Oh, no!" said Emma. She was really worried. "Sheltie! Where's Sheltie? What happened?" Emma frantically looked around, hoping to catch sight of her little Shetland pony.

But neither Sheltie nor Toby was anywhere to be seen. "Where could they be?" cried Emma. There were no gates or hedges to keep them in, just the plain stretching away as far as Emma could see.

"They must have pulled out the peg during the night and wandered off," said Mom.

"But I hammered it in really well," said Dad. He sounded so worried.

Emma felt sick. Her tummy turned a somersault.

Just then, Joshua woke and called from inside the carriage. Mom went in and lifted him out of bed. She stood on the steps, with Joshua in her arms. Emma was close to tears now. She didn't know what to do. She looked from Dad to Mom in despair.

Then Joshua suddenly said, "Sheltie!" and pointed down the road behind them with a stubby little finger. Emma spun around to look where Joshua was pointing.

There she saw Sheltie walking back toward them along the road. In his mouth he held the wooden peg. And on the end of the rope was Toby. Little Sheltie was leading his giant friend like a pet dog on a leash.

"Oh, Sheltie, you clever boy!" yelled Emma. She ran with Dad to help Sheltie bring Toby back.

"What would we do without Sheltie?" said Dad, ruffling Sheltie's forelock. Then he took the lead rope from the little pony and reached up to rub Toby's neck, reassuring him that everything was all right.

Emma threw her arms around Sheltie and gave him a long hug. Sheltie's breath tickled the back of Emma's neck and she found herself laughing. Sheltie pawed at the ground with his hoof and blew a snort at Toby as if to say, "Now don't go off like that on your own again!" Then he looked around at everyone as if he was wondering what all the fuss was about.

Back at the carriage, Dad hammered the big peg in again, but much deeper this time. Then he helped Emma with the breakfast feed for Sheltie and Toby.

Mom was already busy at the little stove inside the carriage, making bacon and eggs for everyone. Then they all sat at the table talking about their route for the day.

The horse-drawn carriage rolled along at a gentle pace. Emma and Sheltie led the way, and Emma talked to Sheltie. She told him where they were going and Sheltie's ears twitched as he listened to every word.

"First," said Emma, "we're going to wind our way down to the coast road and stop for lunch at the Sandpiper Inn. Then we're going to follow the road that eventually leads to Bird Island. Isn't that exciting, Sheltie? A real island. Not just half an island like the one at Horseshoe Pond."

Sheltie raised his head and jangled his bit. He could already smell the sea and took a long sniff through his nostrils. Then he looked back at Toby and blew a snort as if to hurry him along. Toby answered with a deep whicker and quickened his pace.

"That's it, Sheltie," called Dad. "Keep him going."

As the road leveled out onto the flatter coastland route, they suddenly found themselves facing the sea, glimmering silvery blue before them.

Sheltie stopped for a moment and watched the waves breaking on the sandy shore. Seagulls dipped and soared above the breakwater.

Emma stood up in her stirrups for a better look. "Isn't it fantastic, Mom?"

Mom had to hold on tightly to Joshua, who was wriggling like a worm on her lap.

Bird Island sat like a magical mound rising out of the water.

"It looks like something out of a fairy tale, doesn't it, Emma?" said Mom.

"It's beautiful," agreed Emma. She couldn't wait to get to the island and ride Sheltie along its magical shores.

Chapter Five

"Wait until Sally hears about this, Sheltie."
Emma sat back in the saddle and patted
his rump. Sheltie danced on the beach.
He liked the feel of the soft sand beneath
his hooves.

"Look at those two," said Dad. "They're
really enjoying themselves."

"We all are," said Mom, and she gave
Dad a hug. Half an hour later, they stopped
at the Sandpiper Inn. The inn sat right on

the beach and there was a good stretch of sand with patches of grass for Sheltie and Toby to graze.

Wooden tables and chairs were set out on the sand nearby, in front of the inn.

A smiling waitress brought out sandwiches and drinks, and they all sat on the beach and had lunch.

Toby closed his eyes and dozed in the warm sunshine. Sheltie stood close by and sheltered in the cool shadow that his giant friend made for him.

Emma drank her lemonade and stared out across the sea at Bird Island. She imagined that it was her very own enchanted island. And right in the middle, on the highest point, was her fairy castle with a smaller pony-sized castle next to it for Sheltie's stable.

"We'll sit here for a while," said Mom. "Joshua wants to play in the sand. Would you like to take Sheltie for a little ride along the beach, Emma?"

Emma didn't have to be asked twice. She had already leaped up and was calling to Sheltie. Sheltie's ears flicked to attention. He liked nothing more than racing along on soft sand.

"Don't go too far, Emma," called Dad. "And watch out for people on the beach."

"Of course we will," said Emma over her shoulder. Then she urged Sheltie into a trot.

Emma would have liked to ride Sheltie straight across to her island. She had read a book once where a pony had swum into the sea with a girl on its back, riding the waves. But Sheltie didn't seem to be very eager to actually go too far into the water. So they waded a little instead.

Then Emma rode along the wide stretch of beach. Sheltie needed no urging. He was off like the wind, galloping to the rocks right at the end of the beach. Then they galloped back and Emma felt as though they were flying on the wind.

"I went all the way to the end!" yelled Emma.

"I know. We saw you," said Dad.

"If it was a race, you would have won a ribbon," said Mom.

"Sheltie, Sheltie." Joshua laughed over and over as he bounced up and down on the sand.

An old fisherman had been chatting with Mom and Dad about their plans for the weekend.

"We're going over to the island," said Dad. He showed the fisherman the road they were going to take on the map. The road led to a causeway, a long bridge that crossed a shallow stretch of water across to the island.

"It'll be quicker going across the bay. Just here," said the fisherman. He jabbed the exact place on the map with his finger. "The tide will be out until late afternoon. You'll have plenty of time to cross."

"Over the sands," cried Emma excitedly. "I can't wait."

"Are you sure it's safe?" asked Dad.

"Safe as houses," said the fisherman. "Cars go across all the time. Wait for the tide to go out. Then over you go. Takes minutes. Ask anyone. It will save you ages in that carriage."

"OK," said Dad. "Let's do it!"

"There's quite a way to go before we reach the bay, though," said Mom. "We'd better get a move on."

Chapter Six

They set off with Dad driving. Emma
rode Sheltie, and Sheltie showed Toby the
way.

In the distance, Emma saw the causeway.
She stopped Sheltie to point it out to Mom
and Dad.

Because Sheltie stopped, Toby stopped,
too.

"Walk on," said Dad, but Toby wouldn't
move until Sheltie did.

"I don't know who's driving here," said Dad, laughing. "Me or Sheltie."

Sheltie blew a mischievous raspberry and quickened his pace.

"Come on, follow us!" yelled Emma, and everyone laughed. They reached the bay and the carriage rumbled down onto the beach, with the long stretch of sand before them.

The tide was out and Bird Island looked only a short distance away. Toby stepped calmly onto the sand and with no hesitation followed Sheltie at his usual steady pace.

But Sheltie was so excited by the smell of the sea and the softer ground beneath his hooves that he pranced around on the sand. Sheltie really wanted to race across to the island, and Emma had to rein him in and keep him at a steady walk in case Toby decided to do the same. It would have been a disaster if Toby had broken into a gallop.

As Bird Island drew nearer and nearer, Emma felt that she was the luckiest girl alive.

The island turned out to be a truly magical place. The golden beach disappeared away from the shore into rolling sand dunes that were topped with long grasses. Behind the dunes the island rose up through trees into a plump green mound.

On the top of the mound, in the very center of the island, stood a huge gray rock. If you looked up at the rock from a certain angle, it resembled a bird sitting on a giant nest.

"Oh, look!" cried Emma. She was the first one to spot it. "It looks just like an eagle."

Dad parked the carriage and Mom helped Joshua down onto the sand. They all stood looking up at the big stone bird.

"That's why it's called Bird Island," said Dad.

"Funny that you can only see it from here on the island's beach," said Mom.

"That makes it even more special, doesn't it?" said Emma.

Just then, they heard a rumbling noise behind them. As they all turned around they saw the back of the carriage moving away from them.

"The brake!" yelled Dad. "I forgot to put on the brake." Toby had wandered off, pulling the carriage behind him. Luckily, Toby only went a little way before he stopped to drink at a stream that rippled its way down to the sea.

Dad ran over and caught hold of Toby's reins. He tried to pull his head up out of the water, but Toby wouldn't budge. He was a very strong horse.

"Emma!" called Dad. "Bring Sheltie over and get him to lead Toby back. Then we can find a nice spot to camp for the night."

Emma rode Sheltie around in front of Toby. Sheltie seemed to know exactly what to do. He made pony noises to his new friend. And whatever the noises meant, Toby understood and did as he was told. He stopped drinking and let Dad lead him back.

Dad drove the carriage again, with Joshua sitting safely next to him. Mom walked alongside to stretch her legs. Emma and Sheltie led the way as usual, and they went off on a little tour of the island.

On the far side, they found the ideal place to set up camp. Lush grass grew down the hill and spread out like a soft green carpet onto the sands. It was nice and flat with a view across the bay to the mainland. In a few hours the sun would start to go down and they would be able to watch it drop into the sea.

Dad hammered the tethering peg deep into the sand, then set up a barbecue on the beach.

They roasted hot dogs on sticks for their dinner, then afterward played soccer on the beach. Sheltie joined in and chased the ball each time it rolled away down to the sea. Several times, Sheltie accidentally kicked the ball as he ran. Then he learned that if he struck out with his hind legs, he could send the ball flying out backward across the waves.

"Oh, Sheltie!" said Emma. "Don't be so naughty. We'll lose the ball."

But Sheltie just tossed his head and

blew raspberries. Sheltie liked this new game.

"He makes a good soccer player, though, doesn't he, Emma?" Dad laughed. "I've never seen a pony kick a ball before!"

"Sheltie can do anything," said Emma. "But I wish he would kick the ball this way up the beach and stop sending it into the sea."

Emma rolled up her jeans again and waded out for the ball for the third time.

They played for at least another hour before it was time to settle down for the night. Emma laid out some hay for Sheltie and Toby. She pushed the plastic bucket into the sand and filled it with freshwater from the carriage's tank. Then she pushed in another bucket and scooped in some feed. Toby put his nose into the bucket right away and ate it all. Sheltie looked on in disbelief.

"Don't worry, Sheltie," said Emma. "I'll give you yours now." She fed Sheltie, then she clipped the lead rope to his halter and tethered him to the peg alongside Toby.

All the fresh sea air had made Joshua very tired and soon he was fast asleep. Mom tucked him in bed, then sat outside with Dad and Emma to watch the sunset.

"It's a shame we have to go home tomorrow," said Emma. "I could stay here forever."

Sheltie gave a long, loud whinny. "I think Sheltie agrees," said Mom, smiling. "It *is* beautiful here, isn't it!"

The sun turned into a glowing red ball

and they watched it sink slowly behind
the mainland, dissolving into the
glimmering sea.

"Come on, it's bedtime," said Mom.
"We've got to make an early start
tomorrow in order to catch the tide."

"Good night, Bird Island," said Emma.
"Good night, Sheltie." She fell fast asleep
as soon as her head hit the pillow.

Chapter Seven

The next morning didn't begin very well at all. Although Dad had hammered the tethering peg deep into the sand, Toby had pulled it out and wandered off again. Sheltie woke everyone up by snorting and whinnying and making a terrible racket.

They all got dressed quickly and hurried outside to see what the fuss was about. Then they discovered what had happened.

"Good boy, Sheltie," said Emma. She rubbed his neck hard and turned to Dad. "Where could Toby have gone? You don't think he crossed the sands on his own, do you?"

"I hope not," said Dad. "I wouldn't have thought Toby would have wandered off without Sheltie, anyway."

"We'd better start searching," said Mom. "He could be anywhere."

"I bet Sheltie can find him," said Emma. "Sheltie knows where he is, don't you, boy?"

Sheltie pawed at the sand with his hoof.

"Tack him up, then, Emma," said Dad urgently, "and ride around the island. See if Sheltie can find him. I'll climb the hill and try to spot Toby from up there."

"And I'll get everything ready here," said Mom, "so that we'll be able to go as soon as you find him."

"*If* we find him," said Dad. He sounded anxious. "I just hope he hasn't gone too far."

"Don't worry, Dad," said Emma. "Sheltie will find him." She put on Sheltie's saddle, tightened his girth, and fitted his bridle. Soon, Emma was mounted and trotting off with Sheltie around the island.

"Go on, Sheltie," cried Emma. "Take me to Toby! You can find him, can't you?"

Sheltie took a deep sniff and blew a confident snort.

They hadn't been going for very long

when Sheltie suddenly stopped. A clearing to the left of them opened out between two big sand dunes and led away from the beach into the trees.

Emma held the reins loosely and let Sheltie lead the way. Sheltie turned and walked between the dunes into the clearing.

Up ahead, the trees formed a big circle, with a carpet of fresh green grass growing in the middle. Behind the trees, where the island began to rise up the hill, Emma saw the giant shape of Toby. He was leaning against a thick tree trunk, scratching his shoulders on the rough bark.

Emma noticed that the loose rope attached to Toby's halter was tangled in the tree's roots.

"There he is, Sheltie," said Emma. "And look, poor Toby's gone and gotten himself all caught up."

When Sheltie saw Toby, he let out a loud whinny. Toby answered with a series of low snorts and looked over toward Sheltie. Toby seemed really happy to see his little friend.

Emma rode up, then dismounted and untangled Toby's lead rope from the tree roots.

"There!" said Emma as she finally pulled the rope free. "Come on, Toby. Let's get you back."

Emma held the lead rope and Toby followed Sheltie back without protest. He ambled along behind the little pony through the clearing and onto the beach.

"It really is just like leading an elephant,

isn't it, Sheltie?" Emma laughed. Sheltie
shook out his mane. Emma was sure that
he understood what she was saying.

Dad was already back at the carriage.
From the top of the hill, he had spotted
Emma and Sheltie leading Toby and had
raced down to tell Mom.

"If we hurry and get Toby harnessed
quickly, we might just make it across the

bay before the tide starts to turn," said
Dad.

Sheltie and Emma led the way again and
everything was going fine until they were
about halfway across the sands.

Suddenly, Toby stopped and the carriage
lurched to a halt.

"What's happened?" asked Mom.

"I don't know," said Dad. He flipped the
reins across Toby's neck, but Toby wouldn't
move.

"What's the matter with him, Emma?"
said Dad. "Get Sheltie to make him move."

"He can't," said Emma. She was staring
down at the carriage wheels.

"Why not? What's wrong?" Dad handed
the reins to Mom and jumped down.

"The wheels," said Emma. "Look at the
wheels."

Dad looked and saw that the wheels had sunk down into the sand. The lower rims of the back wheels were completely covered. The carriage was really stuck.

Chapter Eight

"We'll have to push," said Dad. "All of us at the back, quickly."

Emma helped, too, and left Sheltie at the front to encourage Toby.

But it was no good. The wheels began to move, but as soon as Toby felt the dead weight of the carriage, he stopped pulling and the wheels rocked back into their deep grooves.

"Go up front with Sheltie, Emma,"

said Dad, "and try again to urge Toby forward."

Emma did, but it was useless. Toby tried his best and pulled as hard as he could. Sheltie coaxed him forward with lots of pony noises. But again, as soon as Toby felt the weight of the carriage behind him, he stopped pulling.

"It's too much for him," said Dad. "The carriage is in too deep."

Then Mom noticed that the tide was coming in. Before, where there had been dry sand, there was now a covering of shimmering water.

"What are we going to do?" said Mom.

"A tractor could pull us out," suggested Emma.

Dad looked at Mom, then turned to Emma.

"OK, then, Emma. Will you ride Sheltie as quickly as you can to the mainland and find help? Stop at the farm we passed on the way over. They're bound to have a tractor."

"I'll be as quick as I can," said Emma.

She felt really nervous, but she was going to do her best. It wasn't very far to the mainland. They were halfway there already. Emma was determined to bring help.

Emma turned Sheltie's head and set off at a canter toward the mainland on the rescue mission.

The first building Emma came to wasn't a farm at all but a small house. Emma jumped off Sheltie at the gate, ran with him up the front path, and hammered on the door.

There was no answer.

Emma knocked on the door again.

"Please come. Please, please come," she
whispered to herself. But no one did.
Sheltie let out a loud whinny. If anyone
was at home they would have heard *that*!

Emma ran Sheltie back down the path as
the first drops of rain began to fall.

At the gate she jumped into the saddle
and Sheltie set off again at a fast trot along

the road. Emma had seen another house right at the top of the hill.

"If we can find a way up there, Sheltie, maybe someone will be in this time."

Sheltie shook the raindrops from his mane and trotted on.

They followed a steep track leading up the hill. The rain was a steady drizzle now, but Emma didn't care. She noticed tractor wheel marks deep in the mud and her heart lifted.

"That's what we're looking for, Sheltie — a tractor. A tractor that will pull the carriage out of the sand."

But the track stopped suddenly and Emma couldn't see the way up to the house.

Sheltie seemed to know where he was going, though. Emma relaxed her hold on

the reins and Sheltie walked around a low
wall onto a second track. This track led
straight up a slope to the house.

The house was a square-built farmhouse.
And in the front yard stood a tractor.

"This is the farm Dad saw!" said Emma.
Sheltie lifted his head and snorted loudly.
He was as excited as Emma.

Emma rode Sheltie right up to the door
and pounded on it with all her strength.

She waited and waited for someone to
answer, but again no one came. Emma
trotted Sheltie around to the back, but the
farm was deserted. There was nothing but
empty barns and sheds.

"Where is everybody?" said Emma,
frustrated.

The rain had brought with it a bitter
wind. Emma felt cold and damp. She

shivered as Sheltie glanced around at a
sudden noise. It was the sound of a car
coming along the road below. Emma stood
up in her stirrups. She couldn't see
anything because the road curved away
beneath the hill, out of sight — but she
could hear the car. And so could Sheltie.

Emma urged Sheltie back down the
steep path. She leaned back in the saddle
and eased the reins to help Sheltie keep his

footing. Then she started to shout for the car to stop.

Sheltie reached the bottom of the track just as the car sped past. Emma waved and yelled, but the car showed no signs of stopping and disappeared around the bend.

The wind whipped the rain into her face as Emma stared at the empty road in front of them.

"Oh, no, Sheltie," she moaned. "It's gone."

Emma guessed that by now the tide would be well on its way in. She thought of Mom, Dad, little Joshua, and Toby stranded on the sands and choked back her tears.

Then Emma had a thought. If there was one car on the road then there might be another. She rode Sheltie over to the side of the road and waited.

It seemed as if they were there for ages before she saw the next car. It was only a speck in the distance on the long stretch of road. But it was a car. And it was coming their way.

"We've got to stop this car, Sheltie," said Emma. "But how?"

Chapter Nine

Emma made Sheltie stand still at the side of the road. But Sheltie was fidgeting and pulling at his reins.

"Don't be frightened," soothed Emma. "It'll be all right."

But Sheltie wasn't frightened. He seemed to want to stand in the middle of the road. That way the car would see them and not go whizzing past. Emma was sure that

Sheltie was trying to tell her something and let him move to the middle of the road.

The car roared up. It was now only a few yards in front of them.

Sheltie and Emma were very brave and stood their ground. For a moment it looked as though the car was going to hit them. Emma couldn't bear to watch and closed her eyes.

The car screeched to a halt. "What do you think you are doing?" the driver yelled at Emma.

"I need help," cried Emma.

Inside the car were the driver and three other people, two women and another man. Emma quickly poured out her story.

"OK!" said the driver. "You lead the way and we'll follow."

The road ended up in a parking lot at the

edge of the bay. Emma could see a shallow
covering of water lapping across the stretch
of sand ahead. The tide was rising. Then
she saw the carriage, with the sea nearly
halfway up its wheels. And Toby's big
hooves and fetlocks were covered by water.

Mom and Dad had lifted as much as they
could carry out onto the back steps of the
carriage. They had their shoes off and their

pants rolled up. Mom was holding Joshua, who thought it was all a big game.

Dad was just about to unharness Toby and lead him to safety when he heard Emma shouting. He looked up to see Sheltie and Emma galloping toward them, with the rescue party running along behind.

"Good job, Emma!" called Mom. "You made it just in time."

"Let's see what a bit of extra weight will do," said Dad.

Emma and Joshua sat on Sheltie. Joshua kept pulling at his own little riding hat and Emma had to make him sit still. Everyone else went to the back of the carriage to push.

"You keep Sheltie by Toby's head, Emma," said Dad. "And get Sheltie to make Toby pull for all he's worth."

Sheltie put his nose up to Toby's and whickered softly. Toby seemed to understand. And when Sheltie walked away ahead of Toby, everyone pushed. Toby strained forward to follow Sheltie and pulled really hard.

"Come on, Toby, you can do it. You can do it!" shouted Emma.

Sheltie whinnied to encourage Toby forward.

"Keep pushing, keep pushing!," yelled Dad. "It's moving. It's moving!"

Sheltie let out an enormous snort and, with one extra effort from Toby, the carriage came out of the sand.

"Keep him going, Emma. Don't let him stop," called Dad. And Sheltie continued on, leading Toby forward.

Mom jumped into the driver's seat and took up the reins.

"Walk on, Toby. Walk on," Mom called. And the others followed behind, cheering and pushing just in case Toby decided to stop.

They kept going steadily and the carriage rolled to the shore with Toby following Sheltie every step of the way. In

five minutes, they were all safely back on dry sand and crossing to the parking lot.

Sheltie had done it! He had gotten Toby to pull the carriage without stopping once.

Dad couldn't thank the driver and his friends enough for coming to their rescue.

"I don't know what we would have done without you," he said gratefully.

"It's a good thing you had that smart girl of yours and that plucky little pony with you," said one of the women. Then they said good-bye and went back to their car.

It had stopped raining now, but Emma was soaked through to the skin.

She changed into some dry clothes and then they set off to take the carriage back to the farm.

"We're really proud of you, Emma," Mom said. "We can always rely on you and Sheltie in an emergency!"

Sheltie puffed out his chest when he heard his name and Emma clapped his neck and gave it a good rub.

When they returned the carriage, Emma told the farmer what had happened. She remembered every detail. Emma wanted to get the story exactly right for when she told Sally. After all, it had turned out to be the most exciting part of the trip.

Chapter Ten

When they had packed up the car and it was time to go, Emma suddenly noticed that Sheltie was missing. She had left him standing contentedly on his own next to the carriage in the middle of the yard.

"Where's Sheltie?" Emma gasped. After everything that had happened, Emma couldn't bear it if Sheltie had wandered off and gotten lost.

Then she heard a familiar snort coming

from the carriage and raced to take a look. Emma suddenly burst out laughing. Sheltie had clambered up the low steps right into the carriage!

The half door had closed behind him, and Sheltie was standing there with his head poking out of the window as though he were in a fancy stable.

"Come look at Sheltie." Emma laughed. "He's made his home in the carriage, just like we did."

Sheltie's eyes twinkled through his long forelock and he blew a noisy raspberry.

Dad raised his camera and took a picture.

"That's one for the album," he said. "Sheltie the brave! In a stable fit for a hero!"

And with that, Sheltie grabbed hold of

the curtains with his teeth and pretended
to eat them. He yanked so hard that the
curtains closed.

"Oh, Sheltie!" Emma giggled. "You are
naughty at times, but you're so funny."

Sheltie stood with his nose poking
through the fabric and blew a fanfare of
loud snorts.

Even the farmer saw the joke and bellowed like a prize bull.

"I've had all kinds of people come and go in my carriage," he said. "But this is the first time I've ever had a pony passenger."

Sheltie answered with a first-class raspberry and stuck his head through the curtains to take a well-earned bow.

PONY♥DAYS

Look for Sheltie in the next
Pony Days book:

SHELTIE
in
Trouble

All through the walk, Sheltie seemed to
have only half the energy he usually had.
And when Emma and Gregory sat beneath
the sycamore tree at Horseshoe Pond,
Sheltie just stood there with his head low,
looking miserable.

"I don't think Sheltie's feeling very well," said Emma.

"Maybe he's just tired," said Gregory. "His leg looks fine to me."

"It's not his leg I'm worried about," snapped Emma. "He's not well. I know Sheltie. Something else is wrong. Luckily, the vet's coming over this afternoon. I'll ask him. Dr. Thorne knows everything about ponies."

Gregory stared down at his sneakers and suddenly got very quiet.

"I don't think I'll come back for lunch after all," he said.

"You've got to," said Emma. "Mom's making pizza especially for you and, anyway, you're supposed to be spending the day. You told your mother you were."

"But it doesn't really matter, does it?"

let him go off on his own like that, Emma. His mother thinks we're looking after him."

"I couldn't stop him," complained Emma sulkily. "It's not my fault. And I don't like him very much anymore, either," she added.

"No, he's not a very thoughtful boy, is he?" said Mom, eyeing the freshly baked pizza.

Dad came in from the yard for lunch and Mom told him what had happened.

"He's an inconsiderate little boy, isn't he?" said Dad. "But I wouldn't worry too much. There's nothing that can happen to him in Little Applewood. I only hope that the boy learns some manners!"

said Gregory. His face had a funny sneer on it.

All of a sudden, Emma didn't think Gregory was so nice after all.

"I'll walk back with you, though," said Gregory. He switched on his bright smile again. "Then I think I'll go explore the stores in town."

There was nothing Emma could do. After all, she couldn't force Gregory to stay. But she still felt annoyed all the same. Mom was busy making a special lunch, and Gregory wasn't even going to bother to turn up to eat it.

But Emma was more worried about Sheltie now and didn't care if Gregory went off on his own or not.

Later, though, back at the house, Mom was very concerned. "You shouldn't have